The Strongest Girl in the World

written and illustrated by

Sally Gardner

DIAL BOOKS FOR YOUNG READERS

DIAL BOOKS FOR YOUNG READERS
A division of Penguin Young Readers Group • Published by The Penguin Group
Penguin Group (USA) Inc., 375 Hudson Street, New York, NY 10014, U.S.A. • Penguin
Group (Canada), 90 Eglinton Avenue East, Suite 700, Toronto, Ontario, Canada M4P 2Y3
(a division of Pearson Penguin Canada Inc.) • Penguin Books Ltd, 80 Strand, London
WC2R 0RL, England • Penguin Ireland, 25 St. Stephen's Green, Dublin 2, Ireland (a division
of Penguin Books Ltd) • Penguin Group (Australia), 250 Camberwell Road, Camberwell,
Victoria 3124, Australia (a division of Pearson Australia Group Pty Ltd) • Penguin Books
India Pvt Ltd, 11 Community Centre, Panchsheel Park, New Delhi - 110 017, India • Penguin
Group (NZ), Cnr Airborne and Rosedale Roads, Albany, Auckland 1310, New Zealand
(a division of Pearson New Zealand Ltd) • Penguin Books (South Africa) (Pty) Ltd, 24
Sturdee Avenue, Rosebank, Johannesburg 2196, South Africa • Penguin Books Ltd,
Registered Offices: 80 Strand, London WC2R 0RL, England

The Invisible Boy and *The Strongest Girl in the World* • First published in the United
States in 2007 by Dial Books for Young Readers

The Invisible Boy • Published in Great Britain in 2002 by Dolphin Paperbacks • An
imprint of Orion Children's Books • A division of the Orion Publishing Group Ltd • 5
Upper Saint Martin's Lane, London WC2H 9EA, England • Copyright © 2002 by Sally
Gardner

The Strongest Girl in the World • Published in Great Britain in 1999 by Dolphin Paper-
backs • An imprint of Orion Children's Books • A division of the Orion Publishing Group
Ltd • 5 Upper Saint Martin's Lane, London WC2H 9EA, England • Copyright © 1999 by
Sally Gardner

Printed in the U.S.A.
10 9 8 7 6 5 4 3 2 1

Library of Congress Cataloging-in-Publication Data
Gardner, Sally.
Magical kids: the strongest girl in the world and the invisible boy / written and illustrated
by Sally Gardner.
p. cm.
The invisible boy was published in 2002 and The strongest girl in the world was
published in 1999 by Dolphin Paperbacks in Great Britain.
Summary: Two stories about ordinary children who suddenly develop magical powers,
the first, an eight-year-old girl who uses her strength for good instead of for fun and the
second, a boy whose invisibility helps him find his missing parents.
ISBN-13: 978-0-8037-3158-5
[1. Magic—Fiction.] I. Title.
PZ7.G179335Mag 2007
[E]—dc22   2006011907

★

To Diani Belli,

for all her love and friendship

★

1

Josie could do many tricks. She could balance a pencil on the end of her finger. She could pick her nose without anyone seeing. She could tickle the cat until it said *Stop it!* But her best trick happened at ten thirty one Friday morning. It was a trick that changed her life.

It happened on the school playground when Billy Brand got his head stuck in the school railings. His teacher, Mrs. Jones, came to help. It was no good. Billy Brand's head would not budge. The school nurse came to have a look. Billy Brand was going very red. The headmaster, Mr. Murray, called the fire department. The lunch lady put butter on Billy Brand's swollen face, but still he could not squeeze his head through the railings. Billy Brand was well and truly stuck.

All the children crowded around to have a look. This was the best fun they had had all week.

"Will he explode, miss?" asked a little boy.

"Miss, miss, will they have to cut off his head?" asked another.

"No," said Mrs. Jones. "Now, children, please don't all crowd round."

Billy Brand started to cry.

It was then that Josie Jenkins, aged eight and nine months, knew that she could do her trick. She felt a tingle of power run down her arms into her fingers.

She went over to the iron railings and bent them right back. It was like pulling tissue paper apart, easy-peasy. Billy Brand's head was no longer stuck. There was a stunned silence, then a loud cheer. Mrs. Jones couldn't believe her eyes. There stood Billy Brand, a little red in the face, with butter on his ears, but free.

At that moment Mr. Murray came running onto the playground, followed by the fire department. All the children were now trying to see if they could bend the school railings, which they couldn't. Billy Brand was standing in the middle of them looking rather red and silly.

"What is the meaning of this?" said Mr. Murray, looking at Billy Brand. "How did you get free? Mrs. Jones, what is going on here?"

Mrs. Jones, who was quite lost for words, pointed at Josie.

"Well," said Mr. Murray, "is this some kind of trick?"

"Yes, sir," said Josie. "I could see Billy was stuck, so I just unstuck him."

The firefighter was looking at the bent school railing. "Who did this?" he asked.

"I did, sir," said Josie.

Mr. Murray looked as if he might explode at any minute.

6

"Josie," he said, "those railings are made out of iron. No one can bend iron, especially not an eight-year-old girl. That is why I called the fire department."

"Shall I straighten them out again, sir?" asked Josie.

"Don't talk such drivel!" said Mr. Murray.

Josie walked over to the railings and in front of the whole school, in front of the firefighter, she gently put the railings back as they were.

2

That evening Josie was having dessert with her family—Mom, Dad, and big brother Louis. She hadn't told anyone about what had happened at school. She had a small feeling that no one would believe her. Even Mrs. Jones, her teacher, had told the whole class that it was just a trick that Billy Brand and Josie had thought up between them. Billy Brand had had to stand

all afternoon outside Mr. Murray's door. Josie had had to write a hundred times: "I won't do any more tricks."

"You're very quiet, my love," said Dad. "Everything all right?"

"Yes," Josie mumbled. She thought there was a chance her dad might understand about the school railing. He often told her that magic is all around us, except people don't want to see it. But as for Louis, who was twelve and clever, best to keep quiet.

After dessert and TV, Josie went to her bedroom. She just had to see if she could still do her trick. She picked up her bedroom chair. It was as light as a pencil. She was just balancing it at the end of her finger when Louis walked into her bedroom. Usually Josie hated Louis barging into her bedroom. But not tonight.

"Josie, what are you doing?" he said with a laugh. "Trying to be the strongest girl in the world? Come on, put the chair down before you hurt yourself." Josie put the chair down gracefully and with no trouble at all.

"You do it, Louis," she said.

"Oh, give me a break. Pick up a chair! That is so easy, it's sad! But if it makes you happy..."

Louis picked up the chair. It was much heavier than he thought. There was no way he could balance it on one finger. Then he nearly dropped it. Finally he banged it down heavily on the floor. He was not going to let his baby sister show him up. He went over to Josie and patted her on the head. "That's a good girl. Time for bed."

For once Josie was not mad at Louis. She knew her trick hadn't gone away.

3

The next morning Josie was awake and downstairs before Louis. Her dad was eating his breakfast. "Well Josie, my love, off to watch the cartoons?"

"No, Dad," said Josie. "I want to help you at work today."

Josie loved where her dad worked. He owned a small garage where he fixed old cars. She would always take him his lunch on Saturday, and he would push his tools off the bench so that his little princess could sit next to him and not get dirty. But she had never before gone to work with him. That was Louis's job.

"All right," said Dad, "you can answer the phone and make us coffee." It was not quite what Josie had in mind, but it would have to do. She waited all morning until her chance came.

"I'm just going out for a minute with Louis.

Answer the phone if it rings and don't touch anything."

Josie went over to the car her dad had been working on. This was what she had been waiting for. Would her trick work on cars as it had on the school railings and on her chair? She put her tiny arm out and held on to the bumper of the car. Then she lifted. Yes! Yes! She could do it! The car was no heavier than her school backpack. With a bit of careful handling she could balance it on the palm of her hand.

That was how Dad and Louis found her: this skinny little girl in a dress holding up a Ford Cortina.

"Don't move!" screamed Dad. "Louis, call the fire department fast."

Josie carefully put the car down. "Don't call them," she said. "They don't like my tricks."

13

4

The rest of the day Dad and Louis tested Josie's so-called trick. There was no doubt about it. This little girl was amazingly strong.

"You're all very quiet tonight," said Mom as they ate dessert. "Cat got your tongues?"

Dad cleared his throat. "Joan," he said, "there is something we need to tell you."

"Oh Josie," said Mom. "You didn't fiddle with anything in the garage?"

"No," said Dad, "nothing like that. It's just—well—Josie is probably the strongest little girl in the world."

Her mom burst out laughing until tears rolled down her face.

"Oh, Ron, you say some silly things."

Dad gave Josie a wink and she lifted the table up as though it were a book and twirled it around on her finger. Mom sat back in her

chair, as white as a newly washed sheet.

"That's nothing," said Louis with pride. "My little sister can lift a car that would need a crane and—"

"Hold on a minute," said Mom. "Are you telling me that our little girl, who is small for her age, and skinny to boot, who looks as if a gust of wind could blow her away, can lift a car?"

"Yes," said Josie. Then she told her mom about the school railings.

"Well, what do we do?" said Mom. "I mean, who would believe it?"

"We do and say *nothing*," said Dad. "We keep it to ourselves for the time being."

"You don't think she should see a doctor?" said Mom.

"Oh, Mom," said Louis. "Josie's fine. She's just amazingly strong."

"Well, Josie," said Mom, "you're still my little girl, strong or not." And she gave her a big hug.

5

Josie was not looking forward to Monday morning. In a school assembly, Mr. Murray, the headmaster, gave a talk on the wrongs of showing off, and playing silly tricks in the playground. Even her teacher, Mrs. Jones, still seemed to be mad at her. Worst of all, she was now the butt of all the jokes.

"How does it feel to be a hairy strong girl?"

"Hey, here comes Superman's sidekick."

It went on like this all day. Only Billy Brand stood up for her.

Dad was right. Best to keep this trick to herself.

Never had Josie been more pleased to hear the bell ring. There was her mom waiting for her.

"Ready for a snack, love?" said Mom.

"Yes, definitely," said Josie. "It's been a really bad day." They walked out of the school

playground toward the main road. That's when
it happened. That's when nothing would ever
be the same again.

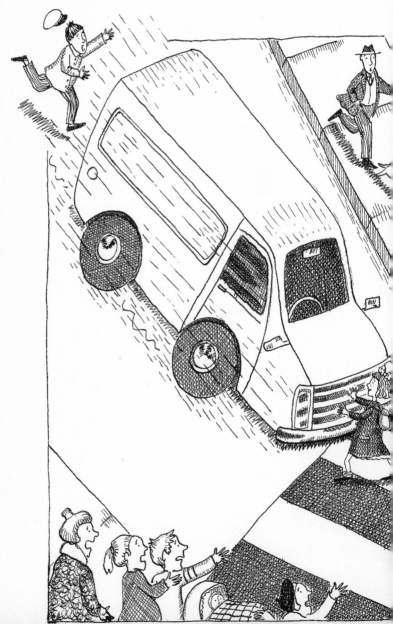

A van came charging out of control down the hill toward the crosswalk, toward Josie and her mom and all her classmates. The driver was running behind it, shouting as loud as he could. Nothing was going to stop it. Josie had that tingling feeling in her arms and without another thought she ran into the road, putting her skinny arms out to stop the van. It was no heavier than catching a football and a lot easier on account of its size. The van stopped in its tracks, no damage done. There was a moment of stunned silence while the crowd took in what had happened. Then chaos. Moms and dads fainted.

The crossing guard went dizzy and the owner of the van couldn't believe what he had seen.

When the police and the ambulance arrived, they thought there must have been an awful accident; there were bodies lying all over the place. The crossing guard was mumbling something about a little girl. The van driver was sitting on the sidewalk saying it must be magic. The poor policeman in charge didn't know what to think. And there standing in the middle of the street was a little girl holding on to a van.

"Are you all right?" said the policeman.

"Oh, fine," said Josie, "but I can't let go because it could start to roll again."

They're all crazy, thought the policeman. He said, "It would be a good idea if you got out of

the road and left that van alone."

Josie did as she was told.

"Now," said the policeman, taking a note-pad from his jacket. "Can anyone tell me what happened?"

But before the policeman could write a line, the van started to roll away again.

Josie ran back into the road and stopped it for the second time.

"Thank you," said the policeman. "Now, where was I?"

It took quite a lot of clear thinking on Mom's part to stop the policeman from taking Josie down to the police station for further questioning.

6

At home Dad was pacing up and down the living room carpet.

"I'm sorry," said Josie. "I just did it without thinking."

Her dad looked up. "Honey, you did the right thing. You are a very brave and strong little girl."

"Nothing will happen, will it?" said Josie, looking at her dad's worried face.

"No, it's just that the newspaper will get ahold of the story and I don't know what they'll make of it."

The doorbell rang. "Hello, Mrs. Jenkins," came a soft-spoken voice. "My name is Avril Ghoast and I'm from the local paper, the *Echo*. I wonder if I could have a word with you about your daughter?"

Josie stood in the living room with Mom and Dad, looking small and worried in a pretty dress and shiny shoes. Avril Ghoast was sure that this was all a huge joke. No one would believe that this tiny wisp of a girl could stop a bike, let alone a van.

"It's a joke, isn't it?" said Avril, looking at Mom and Dad. "Sorry to waste your time. This is my first job as a reporter and I suppose the boys at work thought it would be a bit of a laugh to send me here."

"Well then, the laugh's on them," said Dad.

"Ron, no," said Mom, "I don't think we should say anything."

"It's no good, Joan," said Dad. "It's out now.

The best we can do is let Avril know the true story, not some made-up nonsense."

That is how Avril Ghoast got her first huge break as a journalist. A photographer from the *Echo* came to photograph Josie lifting the Ford Cortina. It was a major headline in the local paper. It was a major headline in the national papers too.

The next day a TV crew turned up to film Josie. The TV reporter wore trendy glasses.

"We need to see this on film," he kept saying. "I mean, how do we know that this isn't a trick?"

"It *is* a trick," said Josie. "It's my best trick ever."

The TV reporter gave a nervous laugh. He turned to Dad and said, "I just got back from India, where I was supposed to film an elephant lifting a car. When I got there, the elephant wouldn't or couldn't do it. I was left with the whole village saying they saw the elephant lift the car on Tuesday, or was it a truck on Wednesday? I came home with nothing. I bet," he added, looking glumly at Josie, "this is just another White Elephant story."

"Can I change before I lift the car again?" said Josie.

"Do what you like," said the TV reporter, fiddling with his glasses. "I'm sure it won't make the slightest difference."

"Well then," said Dad, "I think you'll be in for a bit of a shock."

Josie put on her prettiest party dress, brushed her hair, and put on one of Mom's old hats. When the TV reporter saw her, he didn't know whether to laugh or cry.

"I'm a bit fed up with lifting the same old car. If it's all the same to you, could I see if I can lift a bus?"

"A bus," repeated the reporter. "Why not! Let's do a bus."

They all trooped down to the local bus station. "Which do you like?" said the TV reporter, looking at his watch. "I haven't got all day."

Josie went over to an empty double-decker bus. This would be the biggest test of her trick yet. She went around to the front and lifted it onto her shoulder without any trouble. It weighed no more than an empty backpack. Josie pushed the bus up until she was balancing it on the palms of her hands.

"This is wonderful! Oh my word!" shouted the TV reporter, who seemed suddenly to have come to life. "I am standing in the bus station with Josie Jenkins, who is eight years old and probably the strongest little girl in Britain, in the world, in the universe . . ."

Josie liked this. She took one hand off the bus and straightened her hat. She wanted to look her best. She had never been on television before. The main news story that night was about Josie Jenkins's incredible strength.

7

Stanley Arnold, the strongest man in Britain, was watching the news that night. He didn't find the story about Josie Jenkins very funny. Who was this little girl who had the nerve to go around lifting up cars and buses, that's what he wanted to know. He called his agent. "What is all this nonsense about Josie Jenkins?"

A few squeaks could be heard from the phone.

"I don't care what you say. I want to show everybody that this little upstart is trying to trick us all." A few more squeaks came out of the end of the phone. "No one, I repeat no one, is stronger than Stanley Arnold. I want a competition that will show her up for the fraud she is!"

No one argued with Stanley Arnold. He ate hamburgers by the truckload.

"You don't have to do this silly competition, honey," said Dad.

But Josie was angry. "How dare he say that I'm trying to trick everyone!" she said.

"I'll teach him," said Louis. "He has no right to be so rude about my little sister."

"Now," said Mom. "Let's all just calm down. Josie doesn't have to be in any competition. She doesn't have to prove anything to anybody."

"Especially not to Stanley Arnold," muttered Dad.

But Josie liked the idea of a competition. It gave her a good tingling feeling just to think about it.

Stanley Arnold did some serious bodybuilding. Josie went shopping and bought some very pretty shoes that she had been wanting for ages.

The day arrived. The competition was held in a soccer stadium so that the crowds could get in. Stanley Arnold arrived with his agent, his personal trainer, his publicist, and his fan club. Josie arrived with Mom, Dad, and Louis.

"Well, based on looks alone, we know who's won," Dad said, laughing. "Now Josie, don't go hurting yourself. Stop at any time."

The competition was divided into three parts. First part: dragging a car for ten feet. Second part: throwing a barrel over a wall. Third part: a tug-of-war.

Stanley Arnold went first. He dragged his car, going red in the face, every muscle in his body ready to pop. But he got the car across the finish line. The crowd roared. A commentator said it was Stanley Arnold's fastest time.

Now it was Josie's turn. Sucking a lollipop, she walked over to the car. She had lifted them up lots of times, but she had never *walked* with a car. The huge crowd went quiet. Josie lifted the front of the car and balanced it on one hand, like a waiter holding a tray. She walked past Stanley's car to the other side of the soccer field, still sucking her lollipop. The crowd went wild. Stanley Arnold looked even wilder. The commentator said Josie Jenkins had broken all known records!

Next was throwing the barrel over the wall. This is what Stanley Arnold did best. In fact, he was famous for throwing the barrel. He took a long run, then, with a grunt, let go.

The barrel went high into the air and landed with a loud bang behind the wall. The crowd went crazy. The commentator went crazy. "This is a world record for barrel throwing!"

Then it was Josie's turn. She picked up the barrel and threw it as if it were a tennis ball. The barrel whizzed higher and higher up into the air, so high that it could no longer be seen. Then, like a rocket, it hit the ground, making a huge crater. The crowd was silent. The commentator said in a quiet voice of disbelief, "Josie

Jenkins has broken all known world records for barrel throwing."

The grand finale was the tug-of-war. Stanley Arnold had been sprayed down. He flexed his muscles and put chalk into his hand. Josie just pulled up her socks.

The rope was very thick. Josie took one end

and before she was ready, Stanley gave a mighty pull. Josie landed in the dirt and scraped her knee. The crowd booed.

The referee walked onto the field. Josie pulled herself up. She thought Stanley Arnold was very rude.

"On the count of three, pull . . ." yelled the referee.

One, two, three. Josie grabbed hold of the rope. The tingle in her arms was so powerful that it was like pulling the string on a kite. Stanley Arnold, the strongest man in Britain, felt his feet leave the ground as

he spun around and around the soccer field. It was a sensational victory! There could be no doubt that this was the strongest girl in Britain.

Stanley Arnold got into his large car and went home, saying it was an insult to his strength to compete against a human freak.

8

Josie hadn't changed one little bit. But her life had. Before her trick, there had been time to play with her friends, to watch movies with Louis. Now hardly a day went by without someone wanting Josie to show off her incredible strength.

It had been fun at first. Her teacher, Mrs. Jones, had said she was sorry for not believing Josie, and so had the headmaster. None of the children teased her. In fact, she was quite a star; a star to everyone, in fact, except the person she really wanted to impress—Louis. Why couldn't he see this was her greatest trick ever? Instead, he was constantly putting her down. "Not much skill in lifting cars," he would say, or "You'll end up with muscles like Popeye's."

Louis didn't like Josie's trick one little bit. He was fed up with everyone talking about his baby sister. In truth, Louis was jealous, green with the stuff. Heck, *he* used to be the strong one. He used to be responsible for his little sister. How must he look compared to her, the strongest girl in the world? Only Superman's older brother would know how Louis was feeling. That's if Superman *had* an older brother, which he didn't.

Then came an offer that would change all their lives. Mr. Two Suit flew in from New York just to see the girl with the mighty strength.

The Jenkinses had never met anyone quite like Mr. Two Suit before. He had a face like a potato and a fake flower where his heart should have been.

"The offer," he said, smiling his most charming smile so that his two gold teeth shone, "is this. I take you and your family to New York to do some serious shopping!"

It sounded like a fairy tale. Mr. Two Suit pulled a fat envelope from his front pocket. "Fame and fortune will be yours, Mr. and Mrs. Jenkins. Just sign the contract here, if you please."

Dad signed. How he could he refuse? They'd never been farther than Blackpool.

New York was amazing, with buildings so tall, they could talk to the stars.

"This is cool," said Louis. They were staying in the Plaza Hotel in their very own suite.

"There are more rooms here than we have at home," said Mom.

There were flowers everywhere. A bathtub the size of a swimming pool. Room service at the touch of a button.

"This is the life," said Dad.

Sam Two Suit had gotten Josie a publicist, a clothing designer, a hairdresser, a manicurist, a personal trainer, and a chauffeur with a stretch limo to take them wherever they wanted to go.

Josie was transformed, with puffed-up hair and a frilly, shiny dress. Mom and Dad looked barely recognizable. Louis looked just about all right.

"What have they done to you, Josie? You look like a living doll," said Louis.

Josie agreed, but she wasn't going to let on to Louis. "I think I look pretty," she said.

"Yeah, pretty awful," said Louis.

"That's enough of that," said Mr. Two Suit. "I love it, the camera will love it, and the public will love it. Just think of the Look-Alike Dolls we'll be able to sell."

But Josie didn't feel right. She didn't feel like Josie Jenkins.

The next morning Josie was photographed lifting up a car outside the Plaza. The picture appeared on the front page of several newspapers. The headline read: *Josie Jenkins, age 8, challenges America to find someone stronger!*

10

As it happened, there was no shortage of people willing to pit their strength and their money against Josie Jenkins.

The first of many challenges took place on a beach on Long Island. Josie was dressed in a designer swimsuit and was wearing a hat. She was to beat the record for carrying cement-filled barrels from a raft in the bay back to the shore. Mom didn't like the look of this at all.

"She could drown, Ron," she wailed, "lifting those barrels."

"Joan," said Dad, "for goodness' sake! Josie is going to be fine. What is a cement-filled barrel compared to a car?"

There was only one problem. The raft had been put too far out in the sea. Josie couldn't stand up. However, this was fixed and Josie managed to arrange her cement barrels in neat

building blocks. A crane was needed to take
them down.

"Things are going great," said Sam Two Suit.
"Tomorrow you have a date to pull a truck,
princess. That'll wow them!"

Josie wasn't listening. She was longing to go
swimming with Louis.

"Last one into the sea is a green banana!" she shouted, about to run into the waves.

"Hold it right there, princess," said Mr. Two Suit. "The strongest little girl in the world doesn't play. She trains. That's why I have provided you with a gym and a personal trainer."

Of course, Josie had never used a gym or a personal trainer. It wasn't *that* sort of a trick.

11

It wasn't long before Mr. Big Country himself took up the challenge. He bet more dollars than sense that Josie couldn't lift his horse off the ground.

Quite a crowd turned up on that day, plus a TV crew. This was a story worth filming. Mr. Big Country was big. His horse was big. Josie was small, very small indeed.

Mr. Two Suit rubbed his chubby hands together.

"It'll make a great picture,"

he said. "But next time, I want her in a designer dress."

"It's not the dress that matters," said Mom anxiously. "It's that horse."

"Quit the whining, Mrs. Jenkins, and smile. You're on camera," said Mr. Two Suit, grinning.

Mom couldn't smile. She was far too worried. "She could get badly hurt," she said.

Mr. Two Suit wasn't interested. He was looking at the future. His future paved with gold, with Josie making him the richest man in the world.

The horse turned out to be a calm and well-behaved animal who longed for his owner, Mr. Big Country, to sweep him off his hooves high into the air.

Mr. Big Country puffed himself up like a turkey, then lifted his horse a few inches off the ground. The crowd clapped politely, the horse looked disappointed, and Mr. Big Country gave a satisfied smirk. He was famous for lifting up his horse.

"Beat that, little girl, if you can," he said.

Josie wasn't sure. Her dad tried to sound upbeat. "You can do it, honey," he urged, though to

tell the truth, he could see how Josie might feel
that her trick wasn't up to lifting a live animal.

Suddenly Mr. Two Suit's vision of the future
became horribly clear. He could see himself
losing a lot of money. He wasn't about to allow
this to happen. No two-bit horse was going to
stand in his way to fame and fortune.

"Lift that horse, Josie Jenkins," yelled Mr. Two
Suit. "I order you to lift that horse."

"This is crazy," said Mr. Big Country. "That skinny kid couldn't lift a candy bar. I think you owe me one mighty big check!"

It was at this moment that the horse whispered something into Josie's ear. Then, to everyone's amazement, she lifted the horse by his hind legs as high as she could, which was a lot higher than Mr. Big Country had managed.

The horse snorted. He had waited his whole life for this moment. He reared into the air with Josie holding on tightly and stayed there for what seemed like forever. The crowd went crazy! The film crew couldn't get enough of it. Finally, with a smile, Josie put the horse gently down.

Mr. Big Country looked rather small as he handed over his money to Mr. Two Suit. The horse, on the other hand, was one happy animal. This was something to boast about to his friends in the stable.

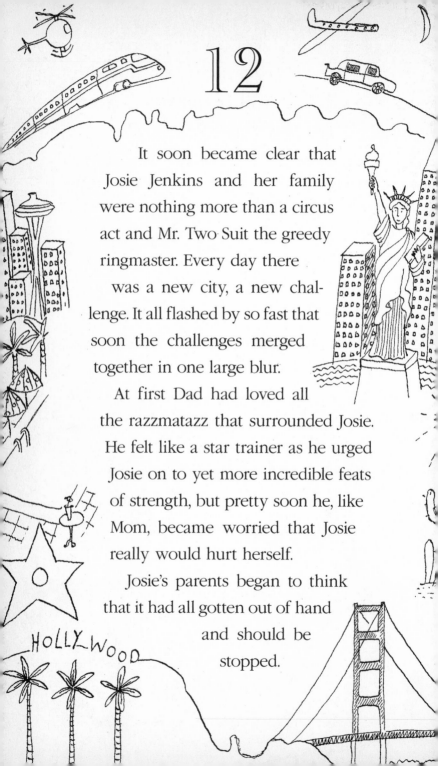

12

It soon became clear that Josie Jenkins and her family were nothing more than a circus act and Mr. Two Suit the greedy ringmaster. Every day there was a new city, a new challenge. It all flashed by so fast that soon the challenges merged together in one large blur.

At first Dad had loved all the razzmatazz that surrounded Josie. He felt like a star trainer as he urged Josie on to yet more incredible feats of strength, but pretty soon he, like Mom, became worried that Josie really would hurt herself.

Josie's parents began to think that it had all gotten out of hand and should be stopped.

Louis agreed. He longed to get back and see his friends and his home again.

He didn't like having to live in the goldfish bowl of publicity. As for Josie, the star of it all, what she wanted was to do something useful rather than these endless challenges that helped no one. Superman saved people, didn't he? The world, the universe, that sort of thing. He hadn't ended up as part of a circus act. If this was all she could do, she would rather go home.

"How is it that such a great trick can go so wrong?" she asked Louis gloomily. They were in their hotel room listening to Mom and Dad arguing next door.

Mom was saying, "Enough is enough, Ron."

Then more muffled words from Dad.

"And what about the garage?" said Mom. "You'll lose all your customers if they find that their cars haven't been fixed."

"I know," shouted Dad. "But what can we do?"

What they did was tell Mr. Two Suit they were going home.

13

"Home!" said Mr. Two Suit, rolling the sound in his mouth like a gobstopper. "Home," he repeated slowly as if waiting for it to change color. He glowered at Josie. "You can't," he said flatly. "I own you, all of you. I own Josie Jenkins Incorporated. You," he said, pointing at Dad, "signed the contract. If you break it, Mr. Jenkins, I'll sue you for every penny you have. Do you understand?"

They understood, all right. They were well and truly caught in Mr. Two Suit's net. In no time at all, he had Mom and Dad bundled off to Florida to a Home for Irritating and Worrisome Parents. They didn't even get the chance to say good-bye. Louis was allowed to stay with Josie as long as he was good.

So here they were, stuck on the twelfth floor of the Plaza Hotel, Louis and Josie by themselves and with no way of getting home.

Josie looked miserable and Louis gave her a hug.

"Don't worry," he said. "We're in this together. And somehow we are going to get *out* together."

14

Louis had a plan. It was quite simple. At the first opportunity, Josie would talk to the TV reporters and tell them what had happened, and how they wanted their mom and dad back so that they could go home.

The next day Mr. Two Suit came in. He was very excited.

"I have a major deal! A cereal company wants you to star in their commercial. All you have to do is lift this three-story house and move it to a new site."

"Why?" said Louis. "That sounds dumb."

"Look, wise guy, I'm getting pretty sick of you," said Mr. Two Suit. "If you can't put a sock in it, I'll send you away like I did your parents."

"No!" shrieked Josie.

"Sorry," said Louis.

Mr. Two Suit turned to Josie. "Filming starts

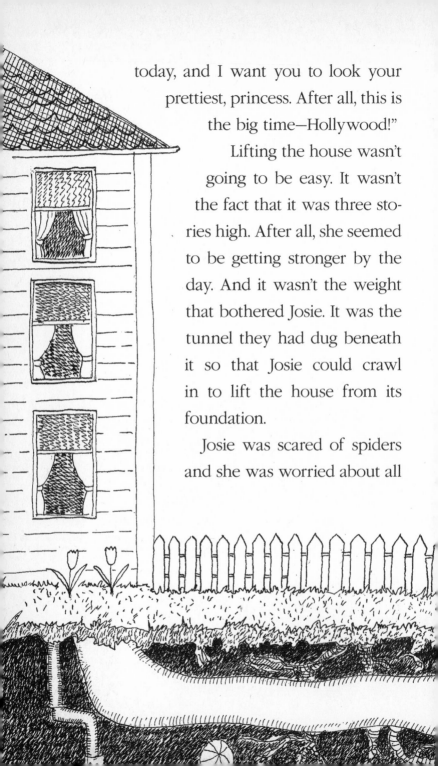

today, and I want you to look your prettiest, princess. After all, this is the big time—Hollywood!"

Lifting the house wasn't going to be easy. It wasn't the fact that it was three stories high. After all, she seemed to be getting stronger by the day. And it wasn't the weight that bothered Josie. It was the tunnel they had dug beneath it so that Josie could crawl in to lift the house from its foundation.

Josie was scared of spiders and she was worried about all

the crawly insects that would appear, like when you lift up a stone. Mr. Two Suit couldn't care less.

"For heaven's sake, what's your problem? How can a few insects frighten the strongest girl in the world? Give me a break!"

"We would like to get started," said the director, "so can we have some action?"

"I'll go in with Josie," said Louis.

"Oh *thanks*," said Josie, taking his hand and giving it a squeeze.

Louis crawled in first with a flashlight to make sure there were no spiders. Josie went in next. He looked at his little sister. She seemed

so small and the house so big. He was just about to say "What are we doing?" when he realized that daylight was shining in.

Josie had the house balanced perfectly on her shoulders. It wasn't heavy, but it was a bit difficult to walk and hold the house at the same time. Louis guided her carefully.

"A bit more this way... yes, you're doing fine."

Josie managed to walk the house down the street to where the very fussy woman who owned it was waiting.

"No, don't put it here, honey. I want it a bit more to the left," she said.

"Look," said Louis. "This is a three-story house my

sister is carrying, not a beach chair."

Josie put the house down without breaking a single windowpane.

"Cut," said the director. "That was just wonderful. The bit with your brother helping was so touching."

"It's in the bag, Josie," said Mr. Two Suit. "The ad company was thrilled. In two days' time, we go to Hollywood!"

Louis and Josie were *not* thrilled. There had been no reporters to talk to, so their plan hadn't worked so far.

"There'll be another chance tomorrow," whispered Louis. "Let's not give up hope."

15

Their chance came sooner than they could have possibly imagined. There was a major disaster. One of the main support cables of the Brooklyn Bridge had come loose! Cars and buses were stuck, no one daring to move in case the whole bridge came down. The television was running updates all day. New York was brought to a standstill. In the Plaza Hotel, Josie and Louis sat glued to the screen.

"All those poor people," said Josie. "What will happen to them?"

"Oh, turn it off," said Mr. Two Suit, "and let's get down to business. We have without a doubt the silliest and easiest challenge of them all. This dad has contacted me and bet half a million dollars that you can't lift his son's backpack. What a punk! It'll be like stealing candy from a baby."

"Why does he want me to do that?" said Josie. "It sounds stupid."

"Because he thinks one day your strength will give out. What a fool."

"But what about those people on the bridge?" said Louis.

"What about them? It means nothing to me. There's no money in people stuck on bridges."

"I'm going to get some sweets from the lobby," said Josie. "Are you coming, Louis?"

Before Mr. Two Suit had time to stop them, the phone rang and he went to answer it.

"This is the plan," said Josie as they were going down in the elevator. "I know it sounds a bit absurd, but I think I could help with that bridge."

Louis had been thinking the same thing until he had seen the pictures on TV. The bridge was an awesome size.

"Oh Josie, that really would be some trick," he said. "But are you sure?"

"Not really," said Josie, "but it's worth a try."

"It sure is," said Louis, smiling.

The lobby was full of people, all milling around, waiting for news about the Brooklyn Bridge. Josie and Louis made their way to a porter. They had decided that he was their best bet because he had a kind, understanding face. At first, he hadn't the faintest idea what these two kids were talking about until it finally sunk in that the little girl in front of him wanted to help. He nearly burst out laughing. Then he looked at Josie again. After all, this was Josie Jenkins, the little girl with the amazing strength. Perhaps it wasn't such a silly idea after all.

"What about your boss?" he asked.

66

Louis begged him not to tell Mr. Two Suit because if he knew that Josie was offering to do this out of the kindness of her heart, he would go bananas.

The porter looked quickly around the lobby, then ushered them into a little room and told them to stay there until he got back.

Louis and Josie waited for what seemed like ages.

"I bet he's called Mr. Two Suit. We'll be in big trouble," said Louis.

Just then the door opened and the porter reappeared.

"Don't say a word," he whispered. "Just do what I say. Mr. Two Suit is on the war path, looking for you."

The porter hurried them out the front of the hotel. To their amazement a helicopter had landed on the hotel grounds. Josie and Louis were rushed into it and the door slammed shut. As they rose high into the sky, they could see the chubby little figure of Mr. Two Suit below, waving his arms.

It gave Josie courage to
see him looking no bigger
than an ant.

16

Garth Griffen was in charge of the rescue services. So far he had the fire department, the police, ambulances, and a number of helicopters at his disposal, but nothing could be done. The whole thing was balanced on a knife edge. If they airlifted people off the Brooklyn Bridge, panic could break out. And if the balance was altered, the whole bridge might collapse. And then there was the tide to think of. Garth Griffen was at his wits' end. The last thing he needed was an eight-year-old girl and her brother on the scene.

"This is a national disaster, not an adventure playground," said Garth.

"I am Josie Jenkins," said Josie very firmly.

Oh, he knew who she was, all right. This was the girl with the mighty strength and the silly dresses. But a car was one thing—this was a huge bridge. Garth Griffen wasn't about to take any chances.

"What I need is some delicate lifting gear, which should be here before the tide changes, not an eight-year-old girl," he said.

At that moment a call came through. There was a problem with the crane. It wouldn't be there for three hours.

"Oh great! Just great!" said Garth. "We don't have three hours. What we do have is a little girl!"

He looked again at Josie. This was madness. Heck,

he was a father of four. He knew all about girls. They could do many wonderful things, but lifting the Brooklyn Bridge? He doubted it.

"Look," said Louis. "I'm not saying she can do it, but it's at least worth a try."

Garth scratched the top of his head. Oh, what did he have to lose? Nothing else seemed to be working.

Josie was put into protective clothing that was too big for her. So was Louis. "I don't leave Josie's side," he said.

"We're a team," said Josie proudly.

They were taken up to the top tower of the Brooklyn Bridge. Josie could see quite clearly where one of the suspension cables had given out. Far down below, the bridge was rocking dangerously back and forth in the wind. The cables were groaning loudly as if about to snap. It was all very scary.

Josie suddenly felt very unsure. The bridge was so massive. Would her trick be up to this?

Louis gave her hand a little squeeze. "Good luck," he said.

At that moment a tingle went down her arms,

even more powerful than the tingle she had
had when Billy Brand got his head stuck in the
railings.

Josie put her feet apart and got ready to pull.
Garth Griffen looked at this little girl, thinner
than a twig, then back down to the bridge. This
was madness. He was just about to say "Forget
it, it's not going to work," when he realized that
little by little Josie was pulling the slack cable
until the bridge was straight.

"Let's get those people off the bridge,"
ordered Garth, "and quickly!"

The bridge was heavy, but not so heavy that she couldn't keep her grip. Far down below, Josie could see the rescue workers getting people to safety.

Louis kept saying encouraging things. "This is a pretty awesome trick, you know," he said. He had never been so proud of her.

Josie kept the bridge straight for a grand total of forty minutes. When she let go, everyone clapped and cheered. Garth Griffen put her on his shoulders and TV reporters rushed up to get the full story.

"How do you feel?" they shouted, pushing their cameras and microphones up to her face.

"I am pleased," said Josie, "that my trick has done some good." Then she carried on bravely, "Ever since I came over here, I have done nothing but silly things."

"But surely," said a reporter, "you're pleased with the fame and fortune that your challenges have brought you."

That was when Louis spoke up and told the reporter how they were nothing more than prisoners of Mr. Two Suit.

"You did it!" said Josie. "You told everyone. Now Mom and Dad will come back and we'll be able to go home."

But unfortunately Louis's appeal for help was cut due to the commercial break.

17

When they got back to the Plaza, Mr. Two Suit looked as if he might explode with rage.

"You go out of the hotel without my permission and fix some piddling bridge that I told you wasn't worth a dime, when we could have made half a million bucks."

They were grounded; locked in their room without dinner, without television, nothing.

They were both feeling very down when the phone rang. Josie answered it. To her amazement, she found she was talking to Stanley Arnold! He was in Florida doing a strong man competition and he had turned on the news and—blow him down!—there was little Josie Jenkins. He was calling to congratulate her and to ask whether there was anything he could do. She had only to ask.

Josie told him all about Mr. Two Suit and what had happened to Mom and Dad.

Stanley Arnold was a man of few words.

"I'll see you tomorrow, kids," he said.

18

The next morning Josie woke up and knew that something was different. She felt strange, heavy, as if her bones were made of lead. She got out of bed and then she knew. Her trick was gone, had disappeared as suddenly as it had come. She couldn't even lift the bedroom chair.

"I can't do it anymore, Mr. Two Suit," said Josie. Mr. Two Suit was not in a listening mood. He just wanted Josie down in the Palm Court in fifteen minutes, looking pretty.

"All you have to do is lift that little backpack," he said.

Josie felt very small. She wanted Mom and Dad. She wanted to go home. When Louis came in, he found her in tears. The minute he looked at her, he knew that something had changed.

"Louis, my trick is gone," said Josie.

"It doesn't matter," said Louis. "At least you won't have to do any more stupid challenges."

Josie sobbed, "I tried to tell Mr. Two Suit, but he wouldn't listen. He said I had to be down in the Palm Court in fifteen minutes. What am I going to do?"

Louis wiped Josie's eyes. "Look, it was a great trick while it lasted," he said, "but you are much more than your tricks, Josie. Don't you see? Mr. Two Suit can't do anything to us now. We'll be able to go home."

Josie brightened up. "You really think so?"

"Yes Josie, I do. I'm glad that your trick has gone away." And he took Josie's hand and together they went down to the Palm Court.

There they found a very tall, pimply boy, fifteen years old, with his very tall father. The backpack was full of large, heavy encyclopedias. When Josie tried to lift it, she couldn't get it off the ground. There was a gasp of disbelief from

the guests who had gathered around to watch.
Mr. Two Suit yelled, "Stop playing around and
lift that backpack!"

Just then, Dad pushed his way to the front of the crowd. Josie couldn't believe her eyes. She ran toward him, tears rolling down her face.

"Dad, oh Dad, I can't do it anymore."

"Never mind, princess," said Dad. "It doesn't matter. Come on, Louis, we're going home."

Dad lifted Josie up and took her to Mom, who was standing at the back with Stanley Arnold. Louis and Josie had never been so happy to see them.

"Oh thank you, thank you, thank you," Louis was saying to Mr. Arnold.

"Very touching," said Mr. Two Suit. "Now, if you would like to step

this way, I think we have some serious talking to do."

Mom, Dad, Josie, Louis, and Stanley Arnold followed Mr. Two Suit into the elevator up to their suite.

"I don't want him in the room," said Mr. Two Suit, looking at Stanley Arnold.

"That's all right," said Stanley. "I'm waiting for a friend, so I'll just stay in the hall until he comes."

"We are going home," said Dad. "We've had enough of your monkey business. There was nothing in the contract about Josie losing her strength."

"Oh, very clever," said Mr. Two Suit. "A short plane ride with Stanley Arnold and you're suddenly experts on contracts. You can leave and go home, by all means, once you've paid the bill."

"What bill?" said Mom. "Josie earned you lots of money. In fact, I think you might owe us something."

"Very funny," said Mr. Two Suit, not laughing. "I have just written out a check for half a million dollars for a backpack. And how much do you think staying in the Plaza costs? And your vacation in Florida, Josie's clothes, her hair, her food, her personal trainer? Who do you think pays for that? *You* do, you idiots."

He handed over a bill. "This is how much you owe me." Mom and Dad turned white. They had never seen so many zeros in their lives.

"There must be some mistake. I mean, we can't possibly owe this much," said Dad.

"Believe me, you do," said Mr. Two Suit.

At that moment, Stanley Arnold entered the room. Behind him stood a very well-dressed gentleman with tiny gold-rimmed glasses.

"May I introduce my lawyer?" said Stanley.

Mr. Two Suit was about to say something but didn't. Stanley Arnold was, after all, very strong. No one messed with Stanley.

"The contract, if you please," he said. Mr. Two Suit handed it over.

"I think," said the lawyer, looking hard at the piece of paper, "that we will talk in the other room."

The Jenkinses and Stanley waited anxiously. They could

hear raised voices, then all went quiet. They were in there for ages. Then the lawyer came back.

"There's bad news and there's good news," said the lawyer. "The good news is that you don't owe Mr. Two Suit anything."

Dad and Mom gave a loud hip, hip, hooray!

"The bad news is that because it was a truly dreadful contract, he doesn't owe you anything either, except your airfare home. I'm sorry that I can't do more for you."

"Oh thank you," said Dad. "It doesn't matter about the money. We just want to be able to leave."

Stanley Arnold shook Josie's hand. "You are a very strong little girl with or without your trick, Josie Jenkins, and I wish you all the best. As for you, young man," he said, turning to Louis, "I take my hat off to you for looking after her so well."

"Hear, hear!" said Mom and Dad.

Mr. Two Suit booked them on to the very next plane to London. He couldn't wait to get rid of them. He had just heard news of a boy in Russia who could fly.

Josie sat in the lobby while Dad went to see if he could find a taxi. No more stretch limos.

"What are all these people doing?" said Mom. Louis looked at the crowd of people coming their way. He recognized the face of Garth Griffen. In the middle of the huge group was a very important-looking gentleman.

"May I introduce myself?" he said. "I am the mayor of New York City."

"Very pleased to meet you," said Josie politely, feeling a bit baffled.

The mayor smiled. "On behalf of this great city, we would like to thank you for your bravery and for your selfless courage in saving so many from a possible disaster."

A loud cheer went up. "To show our gratitude to you and your remarkable family, we would like you to accept this humble check as a sign of our appreciation."

Josie looked at the check in disbelief. There were even more zeros on it than on Mr. Two Suit's bill! Josie jumped up for joy and gave the mayor a kiss. Cameras clicked.

"Thank you," she said. Everybody clapped. It was quite a little party.

They were taken to the airport in the mayor's own limousine and were flown first class to London.

19

It didn't take long for everything to get back to normal. Josie was thrilled to see her house and her friends. She was even excited to go back to school. Billy Brand was pleased to see her and so was Mrs. Jones. They all said that she had been missed. Dad and Mom were their old selves again and Dad's customers forgave him for the late repairs on their cars.

Louis was just pleased that everything was back to how it used to be. It seemed to him that New York had been a dream, except for one thing. He and Josie now got along really well and hardly ever fought. As for Josie, she didn't mind that she was no longer the strongest little girl in the world.

She didn't miss her trick one bit. She was glad to be plain Josie Jenkins, now eight but soon to be nine years old.

It's time to flip the book for another magical story!

It's time to
flip the book
for another
magical story!

The
Invisible
Boy

written and illustrated by
Sally Gardner

DIAL BOOKS FOR YOUNG READERS

★

To Dominic,

with very happy memories of Splodge

★

"I can't believe it," said Mom, opening the gold envelope. "We won the grand prize—a trip to the moon!"

Dad, who was eating toast and reading the morning paper, said, "That's nice."

"Nice!" said Mom. "Charlie Ray, did you hear what I said? We have won a once-in-a-lifetime trip to the moon, all expenses paid, flying first class to Houston, then on the Star Shuttle, and staying in the Moon Safari Hotel, overlooking the Sea of Tranquillity. Oh Charlie, we are the first ones ever to have won this prize!"

Dad dropped his toast and paper.

"Let me see," he said. "Oh, Lily my love, I don't believe it. We are going to the moon!"

Sam walked into the room to find his mom and dad dancing around the kitchen table and singing "Fly me to the moon and let me play among the stars."

"What's going on?" said Sam, who was only half awake and unused to seeing his parents singing quite so loudly on a Saturday morning.

They told him the good news, both excited and talking at once, so it took quite some time before they realized that children under twelve weren't allowed. It meant quite simply that Sam couldn't go.

"Well, that's that," said Dad after Mom had called to double-check with Dream Maker Tours.

"I'll be fine," said Sam bravely. "Look, you must go. It's only for two weeks and I have lots of friends I can go and stay with, like Billy. I'm sure his mom won't mind."

2

The great day arrived. Mom and Dad were packed and ready to go when the phone rang. It was Billy Brand's mother, who was terribly sorry to say that Billy was not at all well. The doctor said he had a very infectious virus. Sam couldn't possibly stay with him now. Mrs. Brand hoped it hadn't ruined their trip.

"What are we going to do?" said Mom, putting down the last of the suitcases.

"I don't know," said Dad.

Just then the doorbell rang. Dad answered it. He was surprised to find their next-door neighbor, Mrs. Hilda Hardbottom, standing there.

"I just popped round to see if you wanted the plants watered while you were away," she said, smiling.

4

"That's very kind of you, Mrs. Hardbottom, but I don't think we will be going after all," said Dad.

"What?" said Hilda, walking uninvited into the hall and closing the front door behind her. "Not going on a once-in-a-lifetime trip to the moon! Why not?"

Mom felt a bit silly. She should have gotten this better organized. "Sam's friend's mom has just called to say he's not at all well, so Sam can't stay there," she said.

"Oh dear," said Mrs. Hardbottom. "Still, that shouldn't stop you. Anyway, you can't cancel, not now, with the eyes of the world on you, so to speak."

5

"We really have no choice. I can't leave Sam alone," said Mom.

"We must phone Dream Maker Tours right away and tell them we can't go," said Dad.

"There's no need to cancel. If it comes to that, I can look after Sam," said Mrs. Hardbottom firmly.

Mom and Dad were lost for words. They felt somewhat embarrassed. Mr. and Mrs. Hardbottom were their neighbors, and had been for years, but they really knew nothing about them, except that they kept to themselves and seemed nice enough.

It was Sam who broke the awkward silence.

"That's the answer, Dad," he said, trying to sound cheerful.

Mom and Dad looked at each other, then at Sam. Oh, how they loved their little boy! It broke their hearts seeing him being so grown-up and courageous.

"It's very kind of you, Mrs. Hardbottom, but—"

"Hilda," said Mrs. Hardbottom, taking control of the situation. At that moment the doorbell rang. "No more buts," said Hilda, opening the front door as if it were her own house.

Plunket Road looked barely recognizable. It was full of well-wishers and TV cameras. Parked outside their front door was a white shining limousine waiting to take the Rays away.

A TV presenter with a game-show face walked into the hall where Mom and Dad were standing. They looked like a couple of startled rabbits caught in the headlights of an oncoming circus bus.

"Mr. and Mrs. Ray, today is your day! You are Dream Maker's out-of-this-world winners!" said the presenter. "How does it feel?"

Dad and Mom appeared to be frozen to the spot.

"Yes," said the presenter, "I too would be lost for words if I was lucky enough to be going to the moon."

Hilda spoke up. "They are a little sad to be leaving their son. But he's going to be fine. Me and Ernie are going to look after him."

The camera panned to Sam's face.

"You must be his kind and devoted granny," said the presenter, pleased at least that someone in the family had a voice.

"No," said Hilda, "I am the next-door neighbor."

The presenter beamed his most plastic smile and his teeth shined like a neon sign. "Now isn't that what neighbors are for!" he said, putting an arm around Hilda and Sam.

Hilda was in heaven at being seen by forty million viewers worldwide. Mom and Dad smiled weakly. Nothing was agreed. This was all moving too fast.

"I brought round a disposable camera," Hilda continued. "I was hoping that my dear friends Charlie and Lily would take some nice pictures of the Sea of Tranquillity, for my Ernie. He wants to know what kinds of water sports they have up there on the moon."

"Well, isn't this cozy," said the presenter, handing the camera to Mom. He was now moving Mom and Dad out of the house into a sea of flashing camera lights, and somehow in all the chaos that was whirling around them, they found themselves parted from Sam. The white limousine whisked them away. The last thing they could see was Sam waving bravely.

There were two things at the top of Hilda Hardbottom's wish list. They had been there for forty years and hadn't until today shown any sign of coming true. The first was to be on TV, the second was to be rich.

"I don't know what's come over you, sweet-pea. You hate boys," said Ernie in a stage whisper after Sam had gone to bed. "You always said they smelled of old socks that had been chewed by a dog."

"There is no need to whisper, Ernie Hardbottom, unless I say whisper," she snapped back at him.

Sam, who was trying to get to sleep upstairs in the cold spare bedroom with no curtains, heard Hilda's voice, and crept to the top of the landing to see what was going on. What he heard made going to sleep even harder.

"Because, you numbskull, how else was I ever going to star on TV?" said Hilda. "You did tape it, didn't you?"

"Yes, every minute of it, dearest," said Ernie.

"Good," said Hilda. Then she added as an afterthought, "Sam's parents must have taken out a lot of travel insurance, don't you think?"

"Well, if they haven't, Dream Maker Tours would have, I imagine," said Ernie, pressing the Play button on the VCR.

"Just think, if anything were to go wrong with that Star Shuttle! Think of all that insurance money," said Hilda, rubbing her hands together with glee.

"That's not very nice," said Ernie.

"Who said anything about being nice," said Hilda, a wicked grin spreading across her face.

Sam went back to his cold lumpy bed. Tears welled up in his eyes. Oh, how he hoped that nothing would go wrong and that his mom and dad would soon be safely home!

The next day Sam went back to school and only had to be with Hilda and Ernie in the evening. All the evenings were long and dull. There was never enough to eat. After dinner they would all sit together watching TV, and Hilda would hand out some of her homemade treacle toffee. The first night, Sam had been so hungry that he had made the mistake of taking a piece. To his horror

his mouth seemed to stick together so he could hardly swallow, let alone speak. All he could do was sit there trying to finish the treacle toffee while listening to Ernie snoring and Hilda's stomach gurgling like an old dishwasher.

Bedtime couldn't come soon enough. Every night Sam would thank the stars that it was one day nearer to his mom and dad coming home.

But then, on the day his parents were due to return to Earth, the unthinkable happened. Houston said they had lost all contact with the Star Shuttle. They were hoping it was just computer failure. The slow, mournful hours passed and the Star Shuttle still couldn't be found. Finally a spokesman for Dream Maker Tours announced on the six o'clock news that the Star Shuttle was missing.

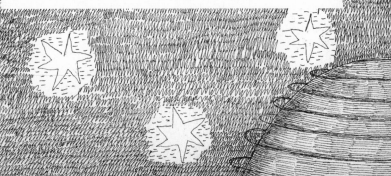

5

The next morning Sam got ready to go to school. He would tell his teachers that he couldn't stay with the Hardbottoms any longer. He had lots of friends at school.

He was sure someone would help him while this terrible mess was being sorted out.

Hilda must have known what he was planning, for she was waiting for him by the front door, wearing her iron face. "Where do you think you're off to?"

"School," said Sam.

"No you're not. It's out of the question. Not at this sad time," said Hilda firmly.

"I can't stay here. I mean, I was only supposed to be with you until my mom and dad got home," said Sam.

"Well, they're not home, are they? So it looks as if you're stuck with us," Hilda said smugly.

"But . . ." said Sam.

"The buts will have to make their own toast," said Hilda, pushing him back upstairs into his room.

The next few days passed in a haze. Hilda wouldn't allow him to go to school, or even out of the house alone, not with all the press and TV camped in their front yard. Sam Ray's parents were a hot story. Sam's picture appeared on every TV, in every newspaper, and on every Internet site in the world. Sam just remembered flashing lights and Hilda and Ernie being called the nation's favorite neighbors.

After a nail-biting week had passed, the officials at Houston said the Star Shuttle had been lost in space. All on board were presumed dead.

That was that. No more exciting pictures to be had. The TV and newsmen packed up and left.

Sam and his parents became yesterday's story. Like the old newspapers blowing around with dead autumn leaves, they were a thing of the past.

6

Hilda had liked the idea of being the nation's favorite neighbor and had made the most of it. She wore a kind and caring face that made the press and friends of the Rays say Sam was lucky to have Mr. and Mrs. Hardbottom to look after him. Especially as there were no living relatives.

But behind the thin disguise, Hilda was making plans. She had rented a cheap bungalow by the sea and made Ernie write a letter to Sam's school saying that they were taking Sam away on vacation, so that he would have a chance to get over his sad loss.

Hilda's plan was simple: She was going to get her hands on the Rays' insurance money. She wouldn't be able to do that if Sam said he didn't want to stay with them, and she couldn't keep him locked up forever. No, the best thing was to get away immediately. There were too many people offering to help. Mr. Jenkins, who had fixed Ernie's Ford Cortina, had said only the other day that he and his family would gladly look after Sam.

Ernie was a bit puzzled as to why Hilda was so keen to keep him.

"Why are you going to all the trouble and expense of organizing a seaside vacation?" he asked. "We never go away."

"Because we can't stay here. People will begin to ask questions," said Hilda firmly.

"About what?" said Ernie, scratching his head.

"About who is going to look after Sam," said Hilda, beginning to lose her temper. "We don't want him saying he doesn't like it here."

20

"I'm sure he doesn't," said Ernie. "We can't look after him. We don't know anything about boys."

Hilda bristled like an old hairbrush.

"I am only going to say this once more, Ernie Hard-bottom, and if it doesn't sink in to that sievelike brain of yours, you can go and live in the potting shed with your CB radio for all I care."

Ernie looked at Hilda. She was not a pretty sight.

"The Rays," she said, talking to him as if he were five years old, "were insured for a lot of money by Dream Maker Tours, and now that they are dead, that money will go to Sam. Or to be more precise, to the guardians of Sam. If we play our cards right, that will be you and me."

"So we're going to adopt Sam?" asked Ernie, still not quite sure what Hilda was up to. "Don't you think, dearest, we are a little too old to be bringing up a boy?"

Hilda looked at Ernie as a cat might look at a mouse. "No," she said. "It means, you peabrain, that we are going to be rich."

"How do you make that out, sweetpea?" said Ernie, looking even more puzzled. "It's Sam's money, after all, and I don't think he would want to give it to us."

Hilda sighed. "I sometimes wonder how, with a brain as small as yours, you manage to keep going at all."

"That's not fair, dearest," said Ernie in a small, hurt voice.

"Oh, for pity's sake. Life's not fair," said Hilda. "It is going to be our money, and once we get our hands on it we are off to where the sun shines bright. Personally I am going to live the life I deserve. Sam can go whistle for his supper, and so can you if you don't step in line."

Ernie knew it was pointless to argue with Hilda. Once she got an idea in her head, it wasn't so much like watching a bull but, rather, a ten-ton truck go through a china shop. Nothing was going to stop her.

7

That night Sam was unable to sleep. He looked out of his curtainless window at the back garden, with its neat rows of pumpkins, its potting shed, and its garden gnomes, lit up in the moonlight. He could even see the tree house that Dad and he had made in his yard next door.

Sam shined his flashlight up into the starry night sky. He had never felt more abandoned.

Space seemed to him so everlastingly vast. Where did it end? He felt tiny and invisible.

Sam lay down and tried to get to sleep. Suddenly there was a loud crash outside.

He sat up in bed. All was quiet in the house. Sam was sure that if it had been an important crash, Hilda and Ernie would be up in a flash, but nothing stirred. Sam looked out of the window again. Everything looked the same, except that something was glowing in the pumpkin patch.

Sam tiptoed past Hilda and Ernie's bedroom. The door was ajar and Hilda's snores were loud enough to cover the noise of the creaking stairs. He went down to the back door and managed with great difficulty to get it open. He felt somewhat stupid standing in the garden, in the middle of the night, in his slippers and pajamas. If he was caught now, he would be in big trouble.

He walked slowly down the garden path. There, among the gnomes and the prize pumpkins, was what looked like a metal salad spinner. A little like the one Hilda used to clean lettuce in, but bigger and a lot fancier. Whirring sounds were coming from it.

Then, to his horror, a gust of wind blew the back door shut. He turned the handle, but it wouldn't budge. He was locked out.

Things were not looking good. This is most definitely a dream, thought Sam. For there, walking around and bowing to the garden gnomes, was an alien with green and splotchy skin, saying, "Hello, I come in peas. Take me to your chef."

When the gnomes didn't reply, the little alien, who was only a bit bigger than them, adjusted the two long pink tufts that stuck out of the top of his head and started again. "Hello, I come in peas . . ."

"Can I help?" asked Sam.

8

The little alien looked up, not in the least bit put off by someone so much bigger than himself. "My name is Splodge," he said. "I am from Planet Ten Rings. I come in peas."

"Good to meet you. I'm Sam Ray," said Sam.

"Are you the big chef?" asked Splodge.

"No," said Sam, "I'm just a boy. I don't cook."

Splodge looked at him and then said, "One milacue, please." He ran back to where the metal salad spinner lay and went inside.

"If this is a dream," said Sam to himself, "then why does it all seem so real?"

"Chief," said the alien, coming out, "take me to your chief."

"If you mean Mrs. Hilda Hardbottom," said Sam, "I don't think she would be too pleased to see you."

Splodge leaned on a flowerpot and muttered to himself. Then, pointing to the garden gnomes, he said, "Who are all those people? Are they prisoners of the Bottom?"

"No," said Sam, "they're plastic, I think, and they don't talk. They're just there to decorate the garden."

Splodge started to make a funny noise, and for one awful moment Sam thought he was choking. He was not up on alien first aid. Then, to his great relief, he realized Splodge was laughing. Sam began to laugh too. Splodge went over to where a gnome was standing and gently pushed him over. He started to laugh again.

"Shh," said Sam, who didn't want Hilda and Ernie waking up. "Why are you here?" he asked.

Splodge looked at him as if he had asked just about the silliest question ever.

"Sauce of the tomato fifty-seven," he said.

This was crazy, thought Sam. "You mean ketchup? You have traveled all this way for that?"

"Yes," said Splodge. "I have traveled from Planet Ten Rings to bring home sauce of tomato fifty-seven for my mom as a present for her . . ." He thought hard for a moment. "Her hello-nice-to-see-you day."

"Like a birthday," said Sam.

"What's that?" asked Splodge.

"Oh, you know, the day you were born," Sam said.

"That's it," said Splodge. "A birthday mom present."

"I think you might be in the wrong place," said Sam. "You need a supermarket." He pointed in the right direction. "It's about a mile down the road."

Splodge bowed. "Thankyourbits," he said, walking back toward the metal salad spinner.

"By the way, what's that?" asked Sam.

"A spaceship," said Splodge, disappearing inside. The door shut behind him. Sam waited, not quite knowing what to do. The spaceship started flashing with bright colors. There was an alarming whooshing sound as it started to rise. It hovered six feet off the ground and then crashed back down again. Another loud bang followed, the door slid open, and Splodge came out bottom first. The two tufts on the top of his head were now knotted together.

"Cubut flibnotted," he said.

"Broken?" asked Sam.

The little alien nodded. "Whamdangled," he said sadly. "I need to make spaceship see-through."

"Do you mean invisible?" said Sam. "How can you do that?"

Suddenly a light went on in the house, and the curtains were pulled back to reveal Hilda and Ernie, lit up like figures in a puppet show.

Splodge froze in fright. He had never seen such a scary sight before.

"That's the Bottoms hard?" he said.

"Yes," gulped Sam.

He looked down at Splodge, but to his surprise and alarm he had disappeared. Sam felt very scared, standing there all alone in the garden in the middle of the night in his robe and slippers. How was he going to explain his way out of this one? His legs began to shake. Then to Sam's surprise he heard Splodge's voice.

"Hurry up," he said urgently. "It's invisible time."

"What?" said Sam. He couldn't see Splodge, but could feel something pulling on his pajama bottoms.

"Hurry up," said Splodge again, "or you'll be whamdangled."

It was too late. The back door opened and there stood Ernie in his rain boots and Hilda in her rollers. She looked more frightening than any alien. She was shining a flashlight around the garden. "I think it's the boy out there near the potting shed."

"Where?" said Ernie. "I can't see anything."

"That's because you are a short-sighted nincompoop," she hissed. "If that sniveling, smelly little toerag of a boy is out here he'll be in big trouble."

"What are you doing?" said Splodge to Sam. "Now invisible time."

"I can't," said Sam desperately.

It was then that he felt Splodge press something onto his leg and the next thing he knew, he was completely invisible, except for his slippers, which refused to disappear.

"I think you were seeing things," said Ernie, who just wanted to go back to his warm bed.

"I don't see things," said Hilda flatly. "Put your glasses on, and have a proper look. Come on, I don't want to be standing out here all night."

"All right, all right," said Ernie, taking the flash-light from her. "Oh yes, I think I see something, sweetpea."

"What?" said Hilda, following Ernie.

Sam was frozen to the spot. His slippers seemed to shine out in the moonlight like a neon sign. Hilda and Ernie were moving straight toward him.

"I just . . ." started Sam.

Ernie looked around. "Did you say anything, dear?"

"Don't be stupid, Ernie. Just keep walking," snapped Hilda.

It slowly began to dawn on Sam that he really was invisible and it wasn't his slippers that had caught Ernie's eye. It was the spaceship. Sam started to walk quickly back toward the open back door, his heart thumping so loud that he was sure that even if Hilda couldn't see him, she could hear him. He went into the house, Splodge still clinging to his leg. Once he was safely inside, Sam shut and locked the back door.

10

Splodge stood in the kitchen tapping his foot. "See now you," he said impatiently to Sam, but all that could be seen of Sam were his pajamas and slippers. Sam himself was completely invisible.

Sam was enjoying this and he was beginning to think that being invisible might just be the answer to all his problems. He would now be able to escape from the Hardbottoms and get help. That was until he caught sight of himself in the hall mirror. There was nothing to see. How would anyone know he was Sam Ray if he was invisible?

Suddenly there was a loud noise from behind him. Sam turned around to see Splodge fiddling with a radio. Sam quickly turned it off.

"Flibnotted! Fandangled! Need radio," said Splodge urgently, pulling one of his tufts. "Must understand you better."

Hilda and Ernie were now banging with all their might on the back door.

Sam picked up Splodge and went upstairs to his room and got out his iPod. Splodge put one earpiece in each tuft, then closed his eyes, folded his arms over his fat little tummy, and listened. After a minute or two he started singing at the top of his voice.

"Hip hop it never will stop,
This planet can rock the stars.
Hip hop this never will stop.
We are the men from Mars."

"Not so loud," said Sam desperately to Splodge, who said, "Like the music, dude, it rocks. So tell me, why don't you know how to do visible-invisible? Do you have learning difficulties?"

"No," said Sam, "we humans don't do that." He was beginning to feel a little worried. "What did you put on me in the garden?" he said.

"My one and only patch," said Splodge. "I was going to use it on my spaceship, but when I saw the Bottoms hard, and you not doing any-thing to escape, I did what any other Splodger-dite would have done. I helped you out. Because, my H bean, you had gone and forgotten how to go invisible."

"No," said Sam, "I keep telling you we humans don't do invisible."

"How do you live?" said Splodge with great feeling, as if this was a design error that should have been fixed years ago. "It must be some-thing awful to be seen all the time."

"It is," said Sam.

"To a Splodgerdite," said Splodge, yawning, "being invisible is like moving leglot. It's just what we do."

"Sorry," said Sam, "you lost me."

Splodge lifted one of his little legs and pointed. "Leglot."

"You mean leg," said Sam.

"Yes," said Splodge. "It's easy-peasy, once you get the handangle of it. Like learning languages." He was now making himself a bed in Hilda's old sewing basket. "Next day when the sun comes up to see you," he said sleepily, "I get my spaceship back."

"Will I be visible again tomorrow?" said Sam, but Splodge was fast asleep.

11

Sam woke to find he was quite normal again. He brushed his teeth, washed, and got dressed, thinking all the time how cool it would be if he was really invisible, and went downstairs for breakfast.

He was surprised to see that there were suitcases in the hall, and that Hilda was busy packing cans of food into boxes, which Ernie was taking out to the car. Perhaps, thought Sam, they were leaving and he would finally be able to get away. It was then that he noticed that the back door had a panel missing from it. He was about to ask how that had happened, but the look on Hilda's face told him it wouldn't be a good idea.

"Now listen to me," she said, loading Ernie up with another box. "We are taking you to the seaside for a few days for a vacation."

"I don't want to go, I can't go," said Sam, feeling panicky. "I mean, I don't want to leave my house, in case my mom and dad get back and can't find me."

"He's got a point, lambkin," said Ernie, resting the box on the edge of the kitchen table. "Anyway, who's going to water my prize pumpkins?"

"You keep out of this, Ernie Hardbottom," said Hilda firmly. "Now you listen to me, young man. Your mom and dad are not coming back. Ever. The sooner you get that into your head, the better."

Sam could feel tears burning at the back of his eyes.

"You should be grateful," said Hilda, picking up the metal salad spinner and putting it on top of the box Ernie was carrying, "that we are going to all this trouble just for you."

"There's no need," said Sam desperately. "Why don't you go, and I can stay with a friend?"

Hilda's face twisted into a witchy snarl.

Sam wasn't going to cry in front of her. He looked again at the metal salad spinner. He was sure he had seen it before.

"Where did you get this?" he asked, picking it up.

Hilda snatched it from him. "Stop fiddling, and get out of here before I box your ears, you ungrateful little scallywag." It was then that she let out a small scream. "What have you done to your ear?"

"Nothing," said Sam.

"Shouldn't boys have two ears, dearest?" said Ernie.

"Of course they should, peabrain." She pulled Sam over to the mirror. Sure enough one of his ears was invisible, although he could still feel it.

"Perhaps it fell off," said Ernie. "I think we'd better start looking for it, and then take him to the hospital to see if they can stick it back again."

"Shut up, Ernie, and take that box out to the car," said Hilda, looking at Sam carefully. "Are you playing games with me?" she said, reaching out to touch the missing ear. Sam moved away fast.

"I think Ernie's right, we should stay here," said Sam.

"Oh you do, do you?" said Hilda, folding her arms over her ample chest. "Well, I'm not fooled by your little joke. Now get upstairs and pack, and by the way, if you see your missing ear, bring it with you."

12

Sam's only comforting thought was that perhaps it wasn't a dream, in which case he should find an alien called Splodge sleeping in the sewing basket. To his delight and great relief, there he was, curled up into a ball.

"Good moon to you," said Splodge, stretching out his little arms.

"We're off! Come down here now," shouted Hilda.

"Is that the call of the Bottom hard?" asked Splodge sleepily.

"Look," said Sam, "I don't want to go, but they're taking me to the seaside and I can't leave you here all alone."

"I can't leave my spaceship," said Splodge, "so I suppose this is toodle-oo."

"Then I've got bad news," said Sam. "It's packed in the car that's taking me away. Hilda thinks it's a salad spinner."

Splodge sat up and looked at Sam. "That's a first-rate spaceship," he said.

Hilda's voice had gotten louder and nastier. "If I have to come upstairs and get you, there will be big trouble. Do you hear me, boy?"

Without another word Splodge got up, made his way over to Sam's backpack, and climbed in. "The one good thing is that you're visible again," he said, making himself comfortable.

"Apart from one ear," said Sam, picking up his backpack.

"What's an ear between aliens?" said Splodge.

The Ford Cortina was packed to bursting. Ernie was so small that he had to sit on three pillows before he could see over the wheel. Sam wondered why Hilda didn't just drive, as she was the one giving all the directions.

"You are going too fast, keep over to the left, no you shouldn't be in that gear."

All Ernie would say was a feeble, "Yes dear, no dear."

It took the best part of a day to get to Skipton-on-Sea and when they finally arrived, smoke was coming out of the hood of the car. It came to a grinding halt outside a dismal-looking bungalow that smelled damp and was colder inside than it was out. Why anyone would come here for vacation was beyond Sam. His heart sank.

"This will do very nicely," said Hilda.

"Well," said Ernie, "the sea air must agree with our Sam because look, sweetpea, his ear is back again."

"Of course it is," snapped Hilda. "It was only that smelly little toerag's idea of a joke, and I don't laugh that easily."

"No," said Ernie, "no, you don't."

13

It was hard to imagine a more miserable and isolated place. Even when the lights were turned on and dinner was made, it had the feeling of being at the end of the world, and there was no way back.

Sam's room was smaller than the last one, and worst of all, the walls seemed to be made of paper. He could hear every word of what Hilda and Ernie had to say and none of it was good. Finally he could hear Hilda snoring, and he knew it was safe to look in his backpack. He wanted to make sure he hadn't gone completely crazy that morning imagining an alien, and a spaceship that looked like a salad spinner. The thought of Splodge was the only thing that had given him hope as they drove farther and farther away from his home, from all he knew and loved.

Sam emptied his backpack carefully. There was no Splodge. He must have imagined it. He looked again. There were only the few things he had packed this morning. He turned it inside out. Tears started to roll down his face. He should have run away before they kidnapped him. Now Sam was lost just like his mom and dad.

He was lying in bed wondering, if he ran away, would he be able to find his way back, when the bedroom door opened all by itself.

Sam sat up in bed and shined his flashlight. There, slowly making its way across the floor, without anyone helping it, was a bottle of ketchup.

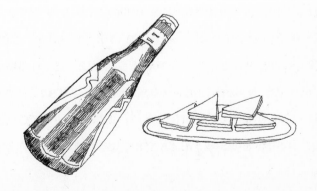

It came to a stop, and then Sam heard the padding of little feet and saw a plate of finger sandwiches wobbling in the air. They tottered one way, then another. Sam shined his flash-light on the plate. A small voice said, "Stop it, I can't see."

"Is that you, Splodge?" said Sam hopefully.

"Who else," said Splodge, becoming visible again, with the plate of sandwiches in his hands. Sam had never been so pleased to see an alien before.

"These," said Splodge proudly, "are for you. Sandwiches of tomato ketchup and pea butter with nut."

Sam was so hungry that he ate them all down. They tasted great.

"Good news," said Splodge. "I have found my spaceship. Bad news, wet inside."

"That's because Hilda thinks it's a salad spin-ner," said Sam.

"It's a Viszler Junior Space Carrier," said Splodge, sounding offended, "and that monster alien thinks it's a salad spinner, whatever that may be."

"It's something you put lettuce in and then you whirl it around and—hey presto—you have clean lettuce," said Sam, finishing the last of the sandwiches.

"Or—hay pisboo—you have a broken space-ship," said Splodge.

"I'm sorry," said Sam.

Splodge didn't look up. He was busy comforting himself by sucking the ketchup out of the bottle.

14

For the first time since coming to stay with the Hardbottoms, Sam didn't feel alone. He sat on the bed with Splodge, looking out the window. The moon looked like a big balloon that had come to rest on the garden wall.

Sam told Splodge about his parents' disastrous trip and how everyone thought they were dead and lost in space.

Splodge tutted. "I shouldn't think so. They most probably got stuck inside a grotter. Has anybody gone and looked?"

"What's that?" asked Sam.

"Surely you know what a grotter is," said Splodge.

"No I don't," said Sam. "I don't have a clue. What is it?"

Splodge looked worried. "Don't you learn *anything* at school?"

"Math, English, history, mainly boring things like that," said Sam.

"Not about the planets, and the stars, and space dragons?" said Splodge. "Or how to look after a grotter, and what to do if an orgback turns up?"

"No," said Sam, who thought he would much rather learn about space than Christopher Columbus.

"Grotters," continued Splodge, "are black as space and hard to see. They have huge tum-tums and float about with their mouths wide open feeding on metricels of light, gaggerling up whatever gets in their way."

Sam looked at Splodge, still not under-standing what he was talking about.

"Planet Ten Rings," explained Splodge, "is milacue. So we look after the grotters and they look after us. Keep the orgbacks away, for a start."

"What are orgbacks?" said Sam.

"Humongous space mon-sters that can gaggerly up whole stars," said Splodge.

"Then why don't you think an *orgback* swal-lowed the Star Shuttle?" said Sam.

"Not possible. They live deep in space and we hardly ever see them. They wouldn't be bothered with a smidger of a thing like a spaceship. It wouldn't be worth munching."

"Would a Star Shuttle be all right inside a grotter or would that be the end of it?" asked Sam anxiously.

"More likely to make a grotter tum feel all wobbly and wonky," said Splodge. "I need to get a message home to my mom and dad. Then I would be able to tell them about the Star Shuttle."

But the problem was, how were they going to do that, now that Splodge's spaceship was broken?

15

The morning did not bring with it a cheerful picture of vacation bliss. A thin drizzle fell and Sam could not see the sea because of a cement wall that blocked out the view. All the neighboring bungalows were boarded up.

Hilda was busy trying to sort out the kitchen. "Did you get up in the night and eat some food?" she said in a menacing voice.

"No," said Sam.

"Well, there are bread crumbs where bread crumbs shouldn't be," said Hilda.

"Perhaps there're mice," said Sam.

Hilda picked up the broom and shook it at Sam. "I don't want any more of your cheek, you little toerag. Go out and play."

"It's raining," said Sam.

"Out!" shouted Hilda.

Sam went out into the backyard. You couldn't call it a garden. It had high walls and crazy paving, and looked more like a prison yard. In it were two broken lawn chairs, a clothesline with a moldy dishcloth hanging from it, and a pot with some tired plastic flowers sticking out of it.

Ernie was in the tiny shed at the back, fiddling around with wires.

"What are you doing?" asked Sam.

Ernie nearly jumped out of his skin. "Nothing, dear, nothing," he said. "Oh, it's you. What do you want?"

"It's raining," said Sam.

"Oh all right, you can stay here, but don't fiddle," said Ernie.

"What's that?" asked Sam, pointing to a funny-looking machine.

"It's a citizen's band radio," said Ernie, beaming with pride as he showed Sam how it worked. "It's not like your everyday radio. Before I retired I used to drive long-distance trucks, and this is

how we talked to each other. We all had different names." Ernie blushed and said, "I was called Tiger Raw. Sometimes if I was lucky, I would be able to pick up signals on it from as far away as Russia and beyond. Isn't she beautiful!"

"Could it send messages into space?" asked Sam eagerly.

"I don't rightly know," said Ernie, scratching

the top of his head. "That's a mighty long way away, isn't it? I mean, it's farther than Russia."

"Only a little bit," said Sam.

"Anyway, I've just bought a bigger receiver," said Ernie, "but I'm having trouble wiring it up. The instructions seem to be written in double Dutch," he said sadly, looking at the manual.

"Ernie, where are you?" shouted Hilda.

"Out here, sweetpea," called Ernie.

"What are you doing?"

"Nothing, dearest, just fiddling," said Ernie.

"Stop it right now," shouted Hilda, "and come in here and help me make pea soup. And you too," Hilda shouted at Sam.

An awful smell of overcooked vegetables greeted them as they walked into the kitchen.

"I want you to stir this," said Hilda, showing Sam a pot of smelly, slimy green liquid. "Don't let it stick to the bottom. That soup is going to have to last us a week."

Sam sighed, and did as he was told. It was then that he realized both his hands were going invisible.

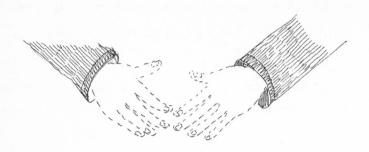

"Hilda," said Ernie, staring at Sam, "do you think boys fade away when they're unhappy?"

"What gibberish are you talking now, Ernie?" said Hilda.

"Sam's hands. They've gone and vanished!" said Ernie.

Hilda turned on Sam. "You are doing this on purpose, aren't you, you ungrateful boy, and after all the trouble we've gone to!"

"I just want to go home," said Sam bravely. "I shouldn't be here."

"He's got a point, dearest," said Ernie.

Hilda looked more frightening than an old flesh-eating dinosaur, all red and furious. "You keep out of this, you peabrain," she snapped, towering over Sam. "You'd better stay in your room until you learn not to play any more of these jokes, or you'll be sorry you were ever born!"

16

Splodge was on the bed, listening to Sam's iPod, and finishing off the last of the ketchup.

"The good news," said Sam, sitting down next to him, "is that Ernie has a radio and a powerful receiver that he can't work. It just might get a message back to your planet. The bad news is, I'm grounded until my hands become visible again."

"It's going to be a long time then," said Splodge.

Sam was slowly fading away. By dinnertime he was completely invisible. All that could be seen of him were his clothes.

"I don't think I should have stuck that patch on you," said Splodge anxiously. "It was meant for spacecraft, not for H beans."

"Stop worrying," said Sam. "Look, last time I came back, so why wouldn't it happen again?"

Splodge tried explaining about invisibility, but it was no use. Sam was far too excited, working out the best combination for scaring the pants off Hilda Hardbottom.

"Hi," he said calmly, walking into the kitchen for dinner. "I am so hungry, I'm almost fading away."

Ernie and Hilda nearly jumped out of their skins when they saw a cap and a pair of shorts coming toward them.

"I don't think this is right, dearest," said Ernie, dropping the newspaper.

"Shouldn't we be able to see him?"

"Of course we should," said Hilda shakily.

"I think it might be best to take him home, and get a doctor to have a look at him," said Ernie.

"What do you think would happen, you ninny, if we went home with an invisible boy?" said Hilda.

"I don't know, sweetpea," said Ernie.

Hilda sat down at the kitchen table. She was really worried. This wasn't in her grand plan. In fact, she could be accused of causing Sam's disappearance. Then they would be in deep trouble. Hilda couldn't allow her plan to go wrong, not now when she was so close to getting what she wanted. Maureen Cook from Dream Maker Tours had said it was only a matter of her seeing Sam, then the money would be as good as theirs.

"Remember the ear, sweetpea, it came back," said Ernie, trying to sound encouraging.

Hilda filled their bowls with slimy green pea soup.

"Eat up," she said, putting on her TV face, "we don't want you fading away altogether now, do we."

Sam took off his cap and put it on the table. Hilda jumped back. There was now nothing to show that Sam was sitting in his seat, except a spoon playing with the slimy soup.

"I don't much like pea soup," said Sam, who was enjoying seeing Hilda squirm.

"What do you like?" said Hilda nervously. "You can have anything you want as long as it helps make you visible again."

So Sam gave her a long list, starting with twelve small bottles of ketchup.

17

That night Hilda couldn't sleep. She was walking up and down in the living room when a picture came off the wall right in front of her, and a china dog started to move across the mantelpiece. Sam was having fun.

"Is that you, Sam?" she said in a shaky voice. Sam didn't answer. Splodge, who was also invisible, was tickling her leg. She let out a scream and Ernie came in, yawning. What he saw made his legs wobbly with fright. A chair was floating around the room.

"That's not right," said Ernie. "I mean, chairs don't do that, do they?"

The chair dropped to the ground with a thud.

"Of course they don't, you ninny," Hilda said, trembling.

"You know, sweetpea," said Ernie, "I think this place might be haunted. I just felt a rush of cold air." The living room door closed with a bang.

Hilda recovered herself. "Of course it's not haunted," she snapped, picking up a pillow and hitting out at thin air. "Take that, you little toe-rag," she shouted. But Sam and Splodge had left, and were safely out of the way in the shed.

"I like being invisible," said Sam. "The only drawback is that it's chilly without your clothes on."

"Pish bosh, you're supposed to come and go, not stay like that all the time," said Splodge. "The sooner we get a message home, the better."

The CB radio was not working that well, mainly because it had been wired to the receiver the wrong way. It took Splodge some time to get it sorted out.

"Come on," said Sam, "I'm getting chilly out here."

"Well, go back to the monster grotto then," said Splodge, "and make us something to fill up gurgling tummy."

The radio was now making strange noises and Splodge kept moving the knobs and listening. Then he started speaking in a language that Sam couldn't understand.

"Χαλλινγ Πλανετ Τεν Ρινγσ."

Sam walked back toward the bungalow. The living room looked as if a giant hippo had had hysterics. Hilda had finally gone to bed exhausted, and was snoring like a battleship attacking an enemy.

The great thing about being invisible, thought Sam, opening the fridge and looking inside, is that I don't feel frightened anymore. I have some power, and that is a truly amazing feeling. He poured out all the milk there was into two

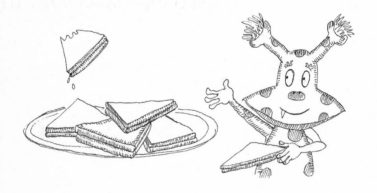

glasses, made a pile of peanut butter sandwiches, and found the last bottle of ketchup.

"I've got a message home," said Splodge, becoming visible again. "They've heard of a sick grotter. In fact, it's caused quite a hollerburluke. Something is definitely stuck inside it. They're on their way out to it. Also my mom says not to worry and sends you her toodle hyes."

"Oh that's wonderful," said Sam. "So what will happen now?"

"Mom and Dad want to say hi and talk to me again tomorrow. Also, I've got to tell them about the invisible problem," mumbled Splodge. "I'm sure my dad and mom can think of something."

18

The bungalow was unusually quiet the next morning. Hilda had taken the car into town to do some shopping, and Ernie was in the shed, playing with his radio. To his delight it was working better than it ever had before, picking up some very strange sounds: "Χαλλινγ Σπλογε Σταρ Σηυττλε ρεχοϖερεδ αλλ ον βοαρδ αρε σαφε."

Sam and Splodge spent the best part of the morning in the living room. Sam was still invisible, but today he was dressed.

It was too chilly to walk

around without your clothes on. They sat together on the beat-up sofa, eating cereal out of the box, watching whatever they wanted on TV.

Ernie, who had been left with strict instructions not to let Sam out of his sight, kept coming in from the shed and saying, "You all right then?" On one of these visits he was sure he saw a green spotty little fellow sitting next to Sam, but then again he might just be seeing things. He didn't have his glasses on, and the next time he looked, it had gone.

At about two o'clock the phone rang. Ernie picked it up. It was Maureen Cook from Dream Maker Tours. She couldn't have sounded more helpful, and said she would be coming down to see Sam tomorrow, to talk about his future.

"That will be nice," said Ernie, putting down the phone and telling Sam what she had just said.

"Do you think she'll recognize me?" asked Sam.

"Oh dear," said Ernie. "Oh dear, I forgot you were invisible."

Hilda was not in a good mood when she arrived home at dinnertime, weighed down by shopping bags. Her mood did not improve one little bit when Ernie told her about Maureen Cook. She started rumbling like an old boiler ready to burst.

"You are worse than hopeless, you peabrain," she said to Ernie, who was looking very sheepish. "What are we going to show her, an invisible boy?"

"Perhaps," said Sam, "if you were kind to me, I might become visible again."

"It's worth a try," said Ernie in a small, shaky voice.

Hilda said nothing, but banged and thumped around the kitchen unpacking the shopping bags.

"Oh that looks nice, sweetpea," said Ernie, seeing all the things Sam had asked for, including the twelve bottles of ketchup.

"Well, none of it's for you," she snapped at Ernie. "It isn't you that's invisible, more's the pity." She handed Sam a bag. "Put these on," she ordered.

In it were a wool ski mask, a pair of multi-colored gloves, a cheap pair of dark sunglasses, and as the finishing touch, a pair of plastic joke lips.

"What are these for?" said Sam, laughing.

"This isn't funny," said Hilda. "Just do as I say."

When he saw himself in the hall mirror he couldn't stop laughing. Oh, now he really did look scary, as if he were about to rob a bank. Can't wait for tomorrow, he thought. How was Hilda going to get out of this mess?

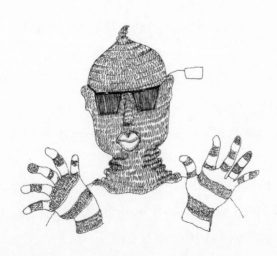

19

The reason, Splodge said, that Splodgerdites adored ketchup was simple. It was the sauce of their good looks—it kept them young, healthy, and wise. Also, growing tomatoes was unheard of on Planet Ten Rings. It was only on Earth that the tomato could be transformed into the right stuff for aliens.

"Have you been here lots of times, then?" asked Sam.

Splodge looked down at his toes. "No," he said, "I have only been here once before with my dad, and it was a short sort of visit."

It turned out that Splodge was only about as old as Sam, and that this was the first time he had traveled on his own to Earth.

"I thought I would get my mom a present," said Splodge sadly, "but it all went a bit star-shaped. I am only a junior space flyer. I start my AST course next year."

"What's that?" asked Sam.

"Advanced Space Travel," said Splodge. "That's when we learn everything to do with space and all the other things like grotters and orgbacks."

Sam didn't want to ask because he had a nasty feeling he already knew the answer.

"Have you ever used one of those invisible patches before?" he said.

"No," said Splodge.

"Do you know what happens when one of those patches is put on a boy like me?" asked Sam.

"No," said Splodge, looking a little shamefaced. "They are only to be used when everything is whamdangled."

Sam was beginning to feel panicky. It was one thing to be invisible for a few days, but not forever. What if his parents came back? How would they know it was Sam if they couldn't see him?

"Will I ever be visible again?" asked Sam anxiously.

"Need to speak to Dad," said Splodge. "I'm sure someone on Ten Rings will know what to do."

But it was proving to be quite difficult to get a message home. Ernie had been fiddling again with the radio and it took Splodge ages to pick up a signal, and then he could hardly hear what they were saying, except for the odd word like

,   ,   .

"We'll have to try again tomorrow," said Sam, seeing the look on Splodge's face. He was tired and his bright green skin was losing its shine.

"Pish bosh, I want to go home," he said sadly. "I miss my mom."

"I know," said Sam. He took Splodge back to the house, gave him a bottle of ketchup, and tucked him in bed.

"So do I," said Sam quietly. "I miss Mom and Dad very much indeed."

20

The next day, the Hardbottoms were up early, cleaning the bungalow.

Hilda put on her smiling face that she kept at the bottom of an old make-up bag and only used for special occasions. Ernie put on his one and only suit. Tea had been set out on a tray in the living room, and the curtains were drawn. Hilda had put Sam in the arm-chair with a rug over his knees. When Ernie saw him sitting there in

the ski mask and dark glasses and false lips, he jumped with fright.

"Hilda," he said, "there's a strange man sitting in the armchair. He wasn't there a moment ago. Did you let him in? He looks very scary!"

"That, you peabrain, is Sam," said Hilda.

When Maureen Cook arrived she was rather taken aback by the Hardbottoms' idea of a vacation. The bungalow was seedy, and smelled damp.

"You could have taken yourselves somewhere nice and hot," she said. "We would happily have paid."

"Didn't want to look too greedy," said Hilda, smiling. "Not until all this is settled, so to speak."

"Please remember," said Maureen, "Dream Maker Tours are here to make your dreams a reality."

"I hope so," said Hilda, taking Maureen through to the living room, and placing her in the chair farthest away from Sam. Hilda handed her a cup of tea and a piece of cake, talking all the time, like a car alarm that wouldn't stop, about how much they cared for Sam and how he enjoyed sitting in the dark wearing a ski mask.

"It makes him feel protected from the outside world. Grief," said Hilda, "can do strange things to one."

"Please, Mrs. Hardbottom," said Maureen, "will you let me speak. Are you feeling all right, Sam?" she asked.

"As I said," interrupted Hilda, "Sam is a bit shy."

Sam nodded and mumbled, "I'm okay."

"Do you like it here?" Maureen started.

Hilda interrupted again. "These questions aren't too strenuous, are they?" she said, sounding concerned. "It's just that we care so much for the boy, and want to protect him. After all, I'm not called the Nation's Favorite Neighbor for nothing."

"Quite so," said Maureen, bringing a picture of Sam out of her briefcase and going over to the window to draw back the curtains. "I would like to see your face, Sam, if you don't mind."

"I do mind," said Hilda, rushing past her and standing in front of the window. "He has been

through an awful lot, why does he have to answer these questions? Isn't it enough that he's
here?"

"I am just doing my job, Mrs. Hardbottom," said
Maureen wearily. This wasn't going according to
plan. She had hoped to have all this sorted out
in no time at all.

"Treacle toffee?" offered Hilda, holding out a
dish. "I made it myself."

Maureen smiled weakly. "Well, one piece if you
insist, then I must ask Sam these questions."

Sam watched a look of horror spread over
Maureen Cook's face as her jaws slowly stuck
together and she was unable to say another
word.

Hilda took her back to the chair farthest away
from Sam.

"Shall we talk about the money?" said Hilda, smiling charmingly.

At that moment Ernie came into the room. "Wonderful news, sweetpea," he said. "The Star Shuttle has made contact with Earth. I just heard it on my CB radio. It looks like Mr. and Mrs. Ray will be coming home after all!"

"Hooray!" shouted Sam, sending the false pair of lips shooting across the room.

Maureen looked startled and Sam put his gloved hand across his mouth and said, "It's the best news ever."

21

Maureen Cook had written out a check to cover their vacation expenses.

"Is that all?" said Hilda, seeing how little she had been given.

But Maureen was now running toward her car, still unable to speak, a hanky held over her mouth.

"Wait a minute, come back," shouted Hilda.

It was too late. Maureen sped off down the road at full speed.

"It's all your fault," Hilda screamed at Ernie. "If you hadn't come charging in like that, we would have been given loads of money."

Hilda marched like an invading army into the shed. She got hold of the CB radio, and lifted it high above her head.

"Don't do that!" shouted Ernie and Sam together. It was too late. Hilda threw it to the ground.

"I think," said Ernie sadly, "you've gone and broken it."

"I hope so," said Hilda. "If you had half a brain, you would have seen what I was trying to do instead of mucking up all my plans."

Hilda went back into the kitchen followed by Sam. All that could be seen of him now was a pair of dark glasses.

"You wretched boy! None of this would have happened if you hadn't gone invisible," yelled Hilda. "Well, you can stop playing games. I haven't come this far for you to ruin everything. You are going to become visible again and tell your mom and dad you had a lovely time with us. Do you hear me?"

Sam, who had long lost his fear of Hilda, said calmly, "I won't. I will tell them the truth—that you are a mean, nasty two-faced witch."

Hilda grabbed a broom. "What did you call me?" she shouted, bringing it down with a nasty crack on the sunglasses, which fell broken to the floor.

At that moment Splodge walked into the room, quite visible.

"I agree," he said.

Hilda dropped her broom and scrambled up on the table as fast as her tubby legs would let her. Splodge went over to where the broken glasses lay and picked them up.

"You," said Splodge, "should be boggled."

Hilda started screaming at the top of her lungs.

Ernie came in holding his smashed radio.

"Look!" yelled Hilda, pointing at Splodge. "It's a monster, a rat, an alien. Don't stand there, do something!"

If Ernie wasn't mistaken, this was the same little fellow that he had seen sitting with Sam the other day on the sofa.

"Well, what are you waiting for? I think that creature has murdered Sam!" said Hilda. "Look at the smashed glasses."

Ernie said nothing. He had seen many frightening things in his life, though sadly none of them as frightening as his wife when she was in one of her moods.

"I can't see what all the fuss is about," said Sam, invisible from the other side of the room. "That's my friend Splodge from Planet Ten Rings, and he's not very pleased that you've ruined his spaceship by filling it with water."

Hilda went white with fright. "Do something, Ernie," she pleaded.

For the first time since he had married Hilda, way back in the dark ages, Ernie felt brave. If a boy and a little alien could stand up to her, so could he.

"No, I won't," he said firmly. "You have gone too far this time, Hilda. I should have had the courage to stop you, but I didn't—more's the pity."

Splodge stepped forward. "You are a cruel and mean hard bottom, and you give Earth H beans a bad name," he said, holding his little hands out before him. Bright green rays came out of his fingertips. Hilda's face went a horrid pink and then became covered in tiny green spots.

"Nice one," said Sam.

Hilda quickly climbed down off the table, ran into the hall, grabbed her coat and hat, stuffed the check into her handbag, and ran out of the front door and down the street as fast as her stumpy legs would carry her.

22

On the TV that night, every show was about the Star Shuttle's miraculous return to Earth. Experts were talking about black holes and all sorts of other theories to explain how a spaceship could disappear for so long. No one mentioned grotters or a small planet called Ten Rings.

Splodge had been spending the evening trying to wire the radio up to his spaceship in the hope of getting a message home, but it wasn't working. Ernie was out in the backyard with the receiver.

"Try it now," said Ernie.

There were a few beeping noises and then nothing.

"Pish bosh, it's hopeless," said Splodge sadly. "We are truly boggled."

"Often when things don't work," said Sam, "my dad gives them a little tap. He says it helps them wake up."

"Go on then," said Splodge.

Sam tapped the top of the spaceship. Nothing happened.

"Well," said Splodge, "it doesn't work."

But that was as far as he got. The spaceship suddenly lit up. Sparks of rainbow color

came shooting out of it, lighting up the drab backyard.

"OW!" said Sam.

Then they all heard:

"Τηισ ισ Πλανετ Τεν Ρινγσ χαλλινγ Σπλοδγε."

"That's my dad!" shouted Splodge. "That's my dad!"

It was a much larger spacecraft that landed in the backyard that night, and Splodge's parents were thrilled to see their son.

"This is Sam," said Splodge, looking down at his toes. Sam held out the arm of his old sweater.

"Oh dear," said Splodge's dad. "What have you done, junior?"

"He was trying to protect me," said Sam. "He didn't realize I couldn't go invisible."

"Sorry, Dad," said Splodge.

His dad smiled a kind smile. "Well, we'd better put it right."

He held out his hands and a blue light flashed around Sam. The next thing he knew, there he was, visible again.

"Thank you," said Sam. "Oh, it's great to be seen again."

Ernie offered to make them tea, but Splodge's parents wanted to get home as soon as possible.

"Wait a minute, I can't go without Mom's present," said Splodge.

He rushed back into the bungalow and brought out twelve bottles of tomato ketchup.

"These are for you, Mom," said Splodge.

She gave him a hug, then thanked Sam for looking after him so well. "He's a bit young to be doing this," she said, waving good-bye. Sam wanted to thank Splodge's parents for helping him find his mom and dad, but there was no time. He was interrupted by the noise of police cars screeching down the road. Splodge just had time to wave before the doors of the spaceship closed behind him. Then there was a whirring noise and in a shower of lights and glitter they were gone, leaving behind Splodge's spaceship.

"Wait!" cried Sam.

It was too late. They were just a spark of light in the distance.

The police were now knocking loudly on the front door. "Mr. and Mrs. Hardbottom," they shouted, "open up in the name of the law."

23

It was the best homecoming ever. Mom and Dad were over the moon to see their beloved boy. They couldn't have been more proud of Sam, and how well he had coped under such appalling circumstances. It was hard to believe that Hilda could have turned out to be so cruel and horrible.

It had been Maureen Cook who had alerted the police. They had arrived just in time to see sparks coming from behind the garden wall.

Mom and Dad felt relieved that it was all over, and they were just happy to be back on Earth with Sam.

The funny thing was they had no memory at all of what had happened to them, except for falling asleep on the homeward journey and waking up again as they were landing. Everyone on board had been most surprised to find out that anything had been wrong, or that they had been missing for so long. Even the officials at Houston agreed that the Star Shuttle disappearance was a mystery.

"It's like it became invisible," said one Houston scientist.

They had driven Sam home in style to his parents, the blue lights flashing all the way to 2 Plunket Road. He had taken with him Splodge's spaceship for a keepsake.

You never know, he thought. Splodge might come back and get it one day.

Ernie had been taken away for questioning, while Hilda was caught trying to get on a flight for Majorca. It was her pink face with its green spots that had given

The Comet

The neighbor from hell

her away. Mr. and Mrs. Hardbottom were both charged with abduction and trying to take money under false pretenses.

Hilda had at last found the fame she had been looking for. Her picture appeared in every newspaper, with the caption "The neighbor from hell." She was sent to prison. Ernie was let off with a warning. The judge felt that if he hadn't been so frightened of his wife, he wouldn't have gone along with her plan.

"What?" said Sam.

"That little fellow Splodge, he asked me something as I was helping him with the radio. He said did I know the meaning of fifty-seven varieties? Do you think," said Ernie, "that he was talking about space and the universe?"

"Ketchup," said Sam.

Ernie looked puzzled.

"That's what it says on the ketchup bottle, fifty-seven varieties," said Sam, and they both burst out laughing.

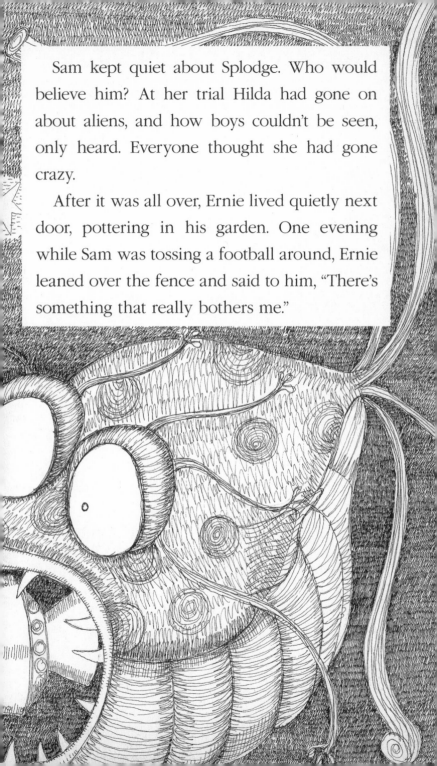

Sam kept quiet about Splodge. Who would believe him? At her trial Hilda had gone on about aliens, and how boys couldn't be seen, only heard. Everyone thought she had gone crazy.

After it was all over, Ernie lived quietly next door, pottering in his garden. One evening while Sam was tossing a football around, Ernie leaned over the fence and said to him, "There's something that really bothers me."